THE SWEETEST DREAMS

WRITTEN / ILLUSTRATED BY BELLA BASHAW

AuthorHouse™
1663 Liberty Drive
Bloomington, IN 47403
www.authorhouse.com
Phone: 833-262-8899

Because of the dynamic nature of the Internet, any web addresses or links contained in this book may have changed since publication and may no longer be valid. The views expressed in this work are solely those of the author and do not necessarily reflect the views of the publisher, and the publisher hereby disclaims any responsibility for them.

Any people depicted in stock imagery provided by Getty Images are models, and such images are being used for illustrative purposes only.
Certain stock imagery © Getty Images.

This book is printed on acid-free paper.

ISBN: 978-1-4772-8625-8 (sc)
ISBN: 978-1-4817-1060-2 (e)

Print information available on the last page.

Published by AuthorHouse 08/26/2023

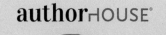

To my mom and my sister. I love you!

Grab your blankie and your bear. Give your loved ones kisses. Tell your pets you love them. Snuggle into your cozy bed. It's time to go to sleep and have the sweetest dreams. When you close your eyes, think about your sweet dream fairies. Right when you start to doze off, they come in with their gentle wings fluttering and sprinkle magic stars. While you sleep, they carry you off to your favorite places.

Sylvia doesn't want to go to sleep. Before she knows it, little dream fairies come to Sylvia's dreams!

In Sylvia's sweetest dreams, Fairies of the night grant her a magic wand. They tell her if her sweet dream turns into a bad dream, the magic wand will protect her.

Sylvia, her doggies, and the fairies of the night love sweet dreams. They dance and fly in beautiful secret gardens that glow. Swirling in radiant joyful peace, they laugh and dance through the night.

The great wise elephant is one of Sylvia's favorite animals. In her dream, he has big fluffy pink wings. She loves to hop on his back and go flying around dream world.

In Sylvia's sweet dreams, she and her doggy swim in beautiful deep blue waters. The sea is filled with hidden treasures and interesting sea creatures.

Sometimes Sylvia's dreams start to turn into bad dreams. " Sharks are coming!" Warn the doggies! "Oh no, Sharks!" shrieks Sylvia!

Just when it seems like the sharks will get them all, Sylvia remembers her magic wand. She calls out her magic word, "WHAMBOOZLE!" Right before her eyes, the magic wand starts to work. Stars and hearts radiate from the wand sending love in all directions!

POOF! Right before Sylvia's eyes, instead of giant sharks coming after her, all that is left is a silly little minnow! The doggies and sea creatures cheer!

Still in dream land, Sylvia and her doggies visit the highest snowiest mountain tops. They ski and snowboard with penguins. Sylvia glides effortlessly through the snow, although the penguins don't seem so graceful! Sylvia watches a penguin go hurling into a puffy pile of snow! She snowboards over to pick up her dizzy penguin friend.

In her sweetest dreams, Sylvia practices spelling and arithmetic. She finds it very easy when the doggies are teaching. 1+1 always equals WOOF!

As Sylvia and the doggies soar through the dreamland sky, they are greeted by bluebirds singing their morning song. That is Sylvia's clue that the sun will be rising, and it's time to return to her cozy bed at home.

And then it's time to start the day. When Sylvia wakes up she smells the pancakes her mom is cooking.

Printed in the United States
by Baker & Taylor Publisher Services